This royally important book belongs to:

_____

_____

_____

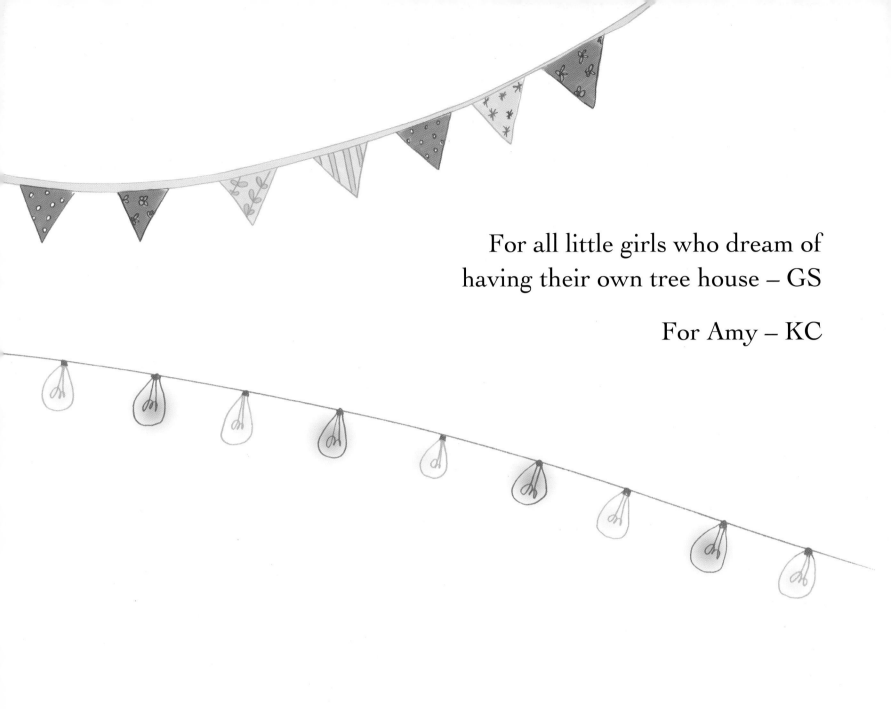

For all little girls who dream of
having their own tree house – GS

For Amy – KC

North Parade
Publishing Ltd

©2021 North Parade Publishing Ltd.
3-6 Henrietta Mews,
Bath BA2 6LR. UK
Printed in China.
www.nppbooks.co.uk

The Treehouse Princess

Princess Esme
and the Royal Secret

Written by Grace Swanton
Illustrated by Kelly Caswell

"It's finished!" Dad called from the garden.

Esme raced outside and three things happened:

🍃 her mouth fell open,

🍃 her legs did a jiggly dance,

🍃 her arms hugged her dad
so hard he nearly fell over.

In the middle of the garden stood
a big old oak tree with crinkly bark.
Nestled in its branches was the most
wonderful tree house Esme had
ever seen!

Before you could say *topsy-turvy*,
Esme was climbing the ladder.

At the top, Esme found a front porch with brightly-filled flowerpots. Miniature roses sat beneath the heart-shaped windows, and a golden doorbell jingled next to the pink door.

Esme wanted to shout, *It's perfect, Daddy, just perfect!* But what she actually said, in a very quiet voice was, *"Wow."*

Then she stepped inside.

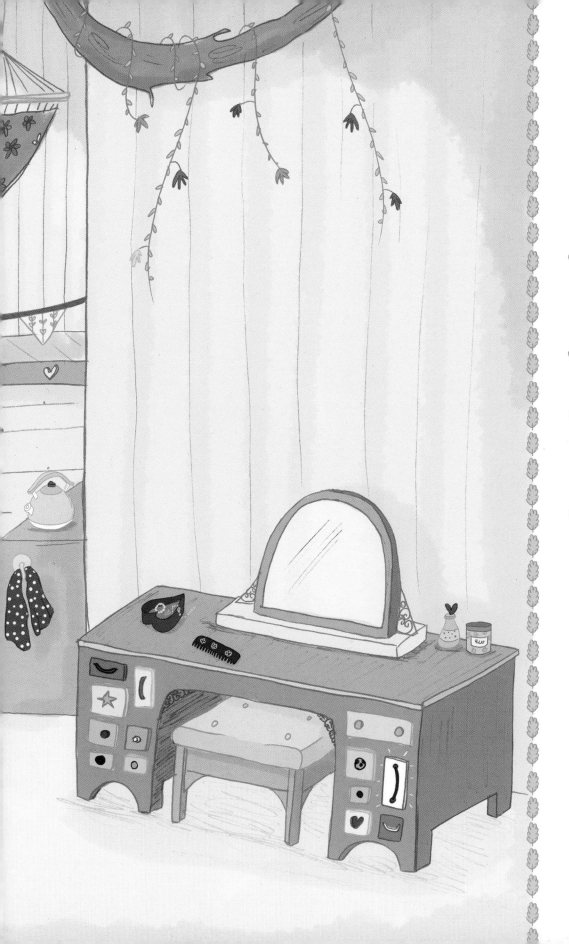

Upon closing the door, Esme saw…

🍃 a crescent moon table with a tiny tea set,

🍃 a hammock for a bed,

🍃 a rainbow rug for the carpet,

🍃 a dressing table with lots of little drawers.

Inside the second-biggest drawer, Esme found her favourite crown. She popped it on her head.

"Hmm," Esme thought next, "I think I'll make a cup of tea."

She turned to fill her kettle with pretend water but the kitchen had disappeared. Instead, Esme was standing at one end of a long, glittering room.

"Princess Esme!" called a voice. "Thank goodness you're here!"

A smiling lady bustled across the room and gave Esme a big, welcoming hug.

"First things first," said the lady, "welcome to Cuddledom Palace. I am the Queen of Hugs."

"Palace?" said Esme.

"Second things second," the Queen continued, "I've lost the King of Cuddles! Would Her Little Highness be so kind as to help me look for him?"

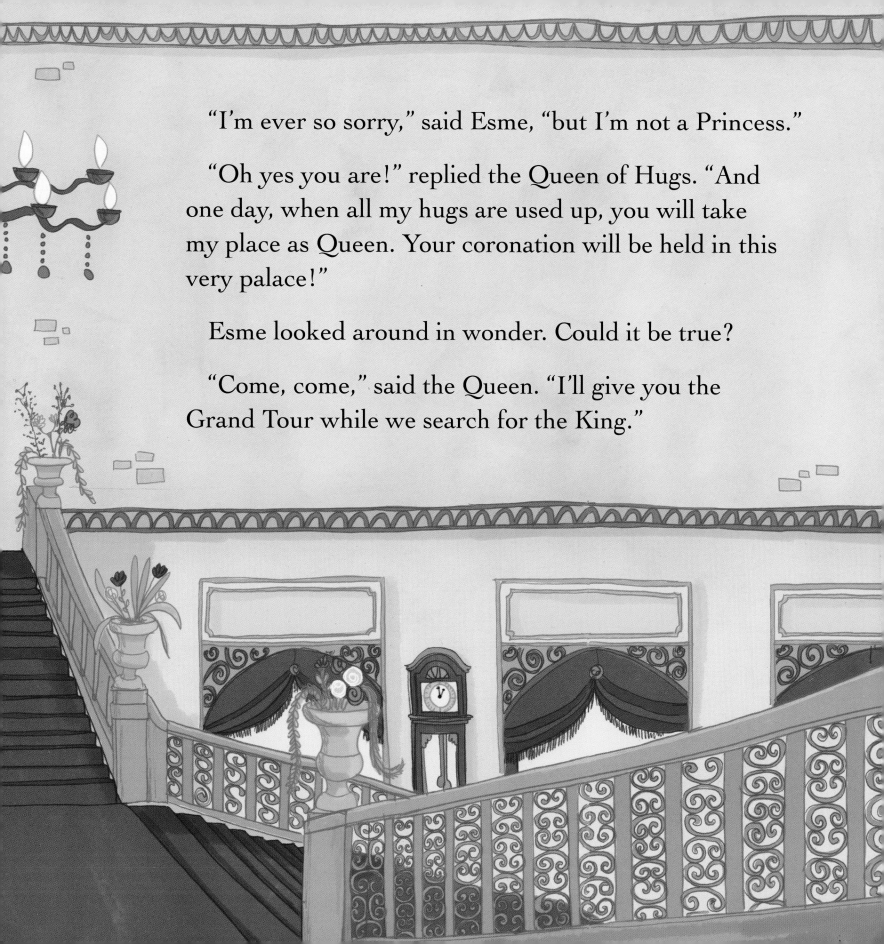

"I'm ever so sorry," said Esme, "but I'm not a Princess."

"Oh yes you are!" replied the Queen of Hugs. "And one day, when all my hugs are used up, you will take my place as Queen. Your coronation will be held in this very palace!"

Esme looked around in wonder. Could it be true?

"Come, come," said the Queen. "I'll give you the Grand Tour while we search for the King."

"May I present your Royal Chamber," said the Queen, "complete with your very own Bathroom Suite."

Princess Esme waited till the Queen wasn't looking, then climbed to the top of a mountain of fluffy towels. She did a **little bounce**...

...then a **not-so-little bounce**...then an **actually-quite-big bounce**. It was springier than the best trampoline she had ever bounced on!

But there was no sign of the King.

Next, the Queen opened the door to the Grand Ballroom. "This," she said, "is where a great many parties will be held in your honour."

The Queen of Hugs pretended not to look while Princess Esme took a long, joyful slide along the perfectly polished floor. It was smoother than the best ice rink she had ever skated on!

But the King was nowhere to be seen.

When Princess Esme did some drawing in the Drawing Room, the Queen joined in. After that, they…

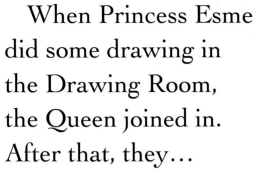

 played Musical Statues in the Gallery,

 tried abseiling in the Library,

pirouetted through the Parlour,

and played hide-and-seek in the Banquet Hall.

But there was still no sign of the missing King.

Finally, the Queen opened the door to the Royal Playroom.

"There you are, Cuddles!" said the Queen.

"Just inspecting the royal trains," the King replied with a grin. "I thought this would be the first place you'd bring Princess Esme. But I see you saved the best till last!"

And, despite having found plenty of other rooms to play in, Princess Esme had to agree that this room was the best of all.

Suddenly, Esme heard someone calling her name. The voice sounded far, far away. Esme ran to the door and opened it.

"Time for tea!" said Mum, peeking around the door.

Esme turned to explain to the King and Queen, but the Royal
Playroom had vanished. The inside of the tree house looked just as it
had earlier, with the kitchen and hammock and crescent moon table.

For a moment, Esme felt sad. Then she smiled. Somehow she knew she would see her new friends again.

Esme took off her crown and put it back in the second-biggest drawer. She climbed down from the tree house and thought about her secret. It was a very royal secret. And it was hers to keep!

The little bell on the tree house jingled, as if it agreed.

Colour in your very
own princess tree house.